Tribute

This biography is dedicated to m
Efendicikoğlu 19th May 1932 – 1(
Akdağ 10th February 1938 their str
Turkish/Greek Cypriot conflict inspired me to preserve those memories and keep them alive.

I also dedicate this to my grandmother Hayriye Osman. Despite her own personal, public and political challenges, she became a strong, powerful and respected female figure in my family.

Family Tree

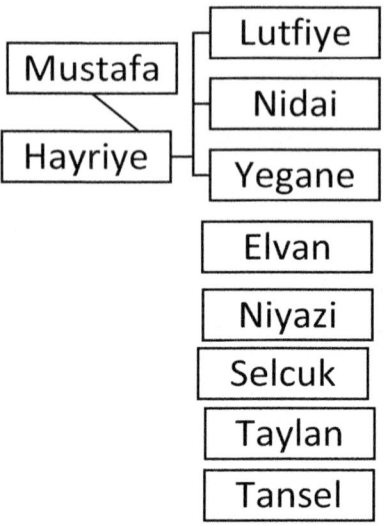

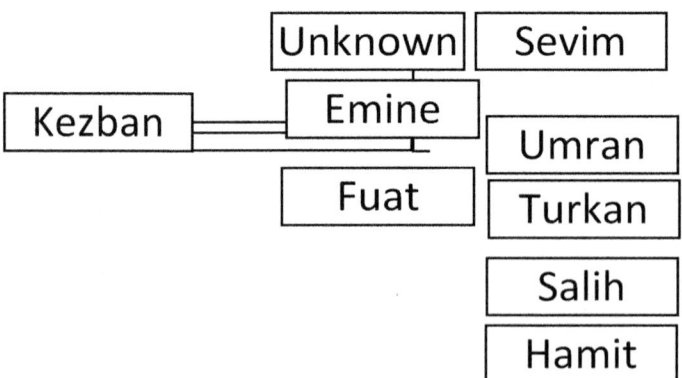

Timeline

1934: – Niyazi Efendecikoglu born in Lefkosa, Cyprus.
1938: – Sevim Akdag born in Istanbul. Turkey.
1939: – Umran is born in Istanbul.
1940: – Turkan is born in Istanbul.
1942: – Niyazi and family move to Tuzla. Niyazi at school.
1947: – Mustafa goes to prison
1948: – Umran dies.
1949: – Hamit is born in Istanbul.
1950: – Niyazi worked at the bakery and forge in the hun.
1960: – Niyazi and Sevim decide to write to one another.
1963:– Niyazi goes to Istanbul to see Sevim.
1964 April: - Niyazi and Sevim get married in Istanbul.
1964 May:-They go to Cyprus for their honeymoon.
1964 December: – Sevim gives birth to twins.
1965 July: – Niyazi and Sevim escape from Cyprus to England.

Guide to Turkish Pronunciation

The letters which may cause problems are shown below with a guide to their correct pronunciation.
All Turkish words and meanings are defined in the glossary.

C as in j 'jam'
Ç as ch in 'chestnuts
Ğ silent, but lengthens like though
I as in build
The İ in Italy
Ö as in urban
Ş as sh in sugar
Ü as in boot
U as in Cup

Chapter 1
Tuzla, Cyprus, August 1964

She clutched the hazed, coloured pearls in her hands, is this what would become of her wedding dress, her dreams and future? Delicately, Sevim tried once more to nip the dress into the only duffel bag she knew she could bring. Trying to be careful of the French lace and trim; she zipped the bag's fine tooth comb. Niyazi touched her right hand lightly, his hands were always cold but with each touch, he could still make her eyes light up. 'You know we won't be able to bring it with us Sevim, Let's just hope we can get out of here alive,' he spoke.

At that moment the bombing in Tuzla began once more for the second evening. Many of the neighbouring Cypriot Turks that Niyazi knew well had been abandoned, killed mysteriously in the night, and left to die on the street. The bloodstained walls outside Mustafa and Hayriye's home on 28 Eylul Sokak were a constant reminder to him of the urgency of leaving. Now with their eight- month baby Hayriye, he knew leaving meant freedom.

The shootings started gradually. Whilst innocent civilians sat in their homes drinking çay and enjoying each other's company, Greek Cypriots would hammer their way inside shouting random orders. Makarios as the Greek Cypriot's archbishop and leader made sure his words had embedded in everyone's brains:
"If Turkey came to save Turkish Cypriots, Turkey would find no Turkish Cypriots to save."[1]
Sevim had been here in Tuzla for little over a year, Niyazi carried her off from her home in Fatih, Istanbul. He offered her the world, London (their future), Cyprus and even Buckingham Palace. Instead she got an overcrowded house of eight siblings who had discarded the place as soon as the Turkish / Greek Cypriot conflict began. This was supposed to be her honeymoon, little did she know that she was caught here, stuck in Tuzla, with one premature surviving twin, no breast milk and a waging war on her hands.

---

1. An undocumented quote by Makarios as interpreted by Turkish President Denktas to Greek Cypriot Leader in 1966.

She had given birth to twins eight months ago, out of respect and love she named the younger and weaker of the twins Hayriye after Niyazi's mother; the older twin Selçuk didn't make it. No one entirely knew why!
Pneumonia was one prediction; the couple were told by the hospital that a hot water bottle given to him for warmth could also have been the cause. It leaked and scolded him severely enough to burn and even kill him.

Now at eight months and still premature for her age, Hayriye was gulping any kind of nourishment down from maize, cereal or whatever formula milk was left on the shelves. Sevim's own breast milk was in short supply because of tensions rising in town and elsewhere in Cyprus.

Chapter 2
Cyprus Tuzla, 1942

Niyazi was the middle child of Osman Efendicikoğlu, but he was popular for being the more placid out of the two brothers. He was the child that was beaten, whipped and hurled across a room for no particular reason. Having been brought up in that fractured relationship with his father, he grew to be accustomed to cowering in front of everyone. As a puny, scrawny child known in the village for his protruding bones and torn shoes, he grew to be a tall, sophisticated, smart, young man with wild, chestnut hair and those obscure, grey, charcoal, coloured eyes.

His mother Hayriye Osman, known to be a strong, hardworking, industrious woman of Tuzla, ran her family of eight militarily. Hayriye's mother Havva forced her to marry young Mustafa, otherwise known as Osman. He was over six feet, tall for a Cypriot Turk. He was Hayriye's first cousin and already married with three children but still Mustafa did not refuse another marriage, another wife.
Hayriye's life and destiny as Mustafa's lifelong married partner paved her life from the start. Hayriye's aunt Emine along with Havva gave her no options. She was forced to bring up his three children before she had hers, an incredibly, minuscule sacrifice that Hayriye had made.

Throughout their marriage, Hayriye would be left alone for months, sometimes years to fend for her children whilst Mustafa was away. In 1945, Mustafa was sentenced to four years for raping two teenage girls. Hayriye's youngest child Taylan was two years old at the time. He was released when she turned seven. As soon as he came back to Hamit Bey Sokak his rage got the better of him, he couldn't remember Taylan at all and assumed Hayriye had had a child whilst he was in prison. Hayriye bared the brunt of his fist and belt for any given situation, accusation or suspicion, she would succumb to his dominant demands, and sometimes would be beaten for just being there.

Mustafa's house in Hamit Bey Sokak was grand for its day; he would brag that his grandfather bought it for a couple of hundred pounds, a hundred and fifty years ago. The house had adjoining shops around it, known as a 'hun'. The shops comprised of a forge and bakery which were on one side of the house. The house itself was not very big but its garden known as

Hayriye's pride and joy and Niyazi's recluse was a new secretive world to hide in.

Niyazi always felt there was another agenda between him and his father. He could never pinpoint why their relationship had always been broken from the start. Maybe Niyazi was too calm and Mustafa mistook this for weakness. Perhaps Mustafa was too forthright and Niyazi perceived it as arrogance, either way, they were trying times for Niyazi to grow up in.

Mustafa's firm hand or his horsewhip would leave the scars on Hayriye's face each time she would stand in the way to take the punishment for her own son. This house provided many tormenting memories of physical and emotional violence, the very ingredients that later made him suffer to the point of being bedridden. Hayriye lost her twin babies as a result of Mustafa's heavy boots when he kicked her down the stairs of Hamit Bey Sokak. However customary it was to behave like a Turkish Cypriot, Mustafa did a lot more than use his whip or fist.

(Niyazi in Middle School)

(From Left to Right, Taylan, Hayriye and Nidai)

Chapter 3
Summer of 1947 Tuzla

Mustafa did not return home for more than two years and Hayriye thought nothing of it; in fact, she revelled and rejoiced in her unclaimed independence and felt relieved to be left alone. He had forced his way into their bedroom on too many occasions leaving her pregnant thirteen times and countless miscarriages.

The eldest lutfiye was now in her teens, she would play the alpha male role in Mustafa's absence. She had a natural skill with knitting and crocheting. Some weekends she would walk to the coast and sell her crochet hats, bonnets, and other accessories along the seafront with Niyazi.
That day past and Hayriye heard the news from neighbours of Mustafa's whereabouts. Hediye was her closest friend, Hedi was her nickname. She would come over almost daily to catch up on any Tuzla gossip. This time, the news was about Mustafa. Hediye and Hayriye's lives were as close as their friendship. Hediye's loneliness ran parallel with Hayriye's life. Hayriye knew almost instinctively when she invited her into her home, the news would be about Mustafa.
'They put him inside this time Hayriye abla be.'
Hayriye's face dropped into her hands, she was sobbing furiously, not that he was in prison, he just hadn't learnt his lesson, and she was left with the burden of finding money to survive. She had some that she saved and hid away from Mustafa, but she would have to rely on Lutfiye, Nidai, and Niyazi. It meant they would all have to work in Mustafa's shops whilst he was away. Hayriye shook her head from side to side whilst patting her knee.
'Offf, off, off'. She cried and the tears started to well in Hayriye's eyes again, Hediye was more relieved at the fact that it was another woman's husband and not her own. Hayriye was to spend the next two years bringing up her children on her own. Lutfiye and Elvan played roles of surrogate mother to the younger girls Taylan and Tansel, they would feed them, dress them, and take them to school. No questions were asked about Mustafa's whereabouts in the Osman family household for another two years and the two women were able to sit on the garden veranda in the blazing sun drinking hot çay and waving their handkerchiefs to cool themselves down.

Niyazi was relieved to wake up to daily, peaceful life and go to school without a single beating in the morning. In fact, Niyazi was able to finish Lise without the constant demands of working in the shops to bring money home, most children were not that fortunate! Although everyone in Lefkoşa and Tuzla knew about Mustafa Osman and the kind of man he was, Niyazi had almost accepted his fate with the kind of father that had brought him into the world.

Niyazi had a love and a curious mind for History. He found himself reading any library book that was given to him. The garden was his haven to read about the political constitutions of Turkey during the Ottoman Empire and Kemalism. Kemalism was a newlyfound word in Cyprus but Niyazi knew exactly what it meant.
'Ben Ataturkciyim.' He would tell his friends with pride.
'Ama Niyazi abi, sen Kibriz Turk degilmisin?' The children would always reply. The children were curious to know the difference. Even back then, however patriotic Niyazi seemed, his humanitarianism ran deeper. He was as proud of his Greek friends as he was with his Turkish Cypriot ones. Niyazi spoke Greek to his neighbours, school friends, and in the bakery when he was working. Suleyman his closest friend was the outcome of a Greek Cypriot father and Turkish Cypriot mother. Suleyman worked with Niyazi in the bakery on odd days after school and weekend, they would weave in and out of both languages whilst speaking to one another as if it was the most natural way to speak. Niyazi admired Suleyman's loyalty and Suleyman thought Niyazi was the most honest person in Tuzla.
Everyone in Tuzla had to rely on one or two teachers to teach a hundred children. Niyazi was fortunate, he was the middle child and was in the same class as Nidai and Elvan.
His teacher Hoca Hasanoğlu was a tall, slender man in his thirties, he was brought up in the village but left for the UK to further his studies. Every Saturday morning was market day on Mehmet Hindiyano Sokak, Niyazi would stroll down there midday after catching some red snipe in Famagusta Bay. He would give Hoca Hasanoğlu a helping hand with the groceries and in exchange, he would treat him to a bottle of gazoz. However, it was more than just help. Niyazi thrived talking to his teacher about Turkish history, he kept all kinds of dates drilled in his mind, the Byzantine-Ottoman Wars, Fatih Sultan Mehmet, Ataturk fighting in the battle of Gallipoli and his strategic methods of keeping his enemies out of Ankara. It was unheard of for anyone in this tiny village to know about the rise and fall of Fatih Sultan Mehmet but these heroic and reverent figures dominated Niyazi's life whom he held in high prestige. Evidently, the man he could admire and respect as the father figure in his life was hardly there.

Niyazi felt taken back on meeting Hasanoğlu the first time that day in the market, how had he remembered him in a crowded, clustered class of a hundred. Niyazi never knew that Hasanoğlu had a similar kind of mutual respect for Niyazi as he did for him. Hasanoğlu would look into Niyazi's anchor, grey coloured eyes, and see his own zealous self to learn and thrive for knowledge. He saw his desperation to leave Tuzla, he would gently pat him on the shoulders, look intensely into those eyes and say.
'Eğitim oğlum eğitim.' Those words were ingrained in Niyazi's mind for the rest of his life. It was the very substance of what he would say to his own children so they could reinforce themselves in British society without prejudice or labels.

Niyazi's Saturday morning was taken up with earning Lira from the red snipes and socialising with Hasanoğlu about his astounding memory of dates. Niyazi was not a man of business ethics and rationale, he was a dreamer. He too wanted to go to the UK to study and travel, he would look at the photographs Hasanoğlu would bring in to the school of the touristic sights of London and many of the children would stare in awe. Niyazi knew that it could be a reality.

His Saturday afternoons were spent sketching portraits of Ataturk and Fatih Sultan Mehmet. He would sharpen his pencil with a kitchen meat knife to shade the dark, rigid lines of the Sultan's distinctive nose and the elaborate fabric of his turban. The Sultan's eyes required precision as each painting illustrated a sense of power, perfection, and purity. He would sit for hours in the half-baked sun and deep, reddening sky. Nidai would be barbequing his favourite şeftali kebab on the skewers. Hayriye would always give extra portions to Niyazi. Her nervous disposition about Niyazi remained unchanged even as a young, bedridden child. Mustafa saw Niyazi as an inconvenience and Niyazi more often saw the result of his sharp, right, hand. Everyone would fall silent whilst digging into the şeftali kebab. That afternoon Niyazi broke the silence.
'Anne' he commanded, 'Tomorrow is school photo day.' He wanted to make sure his shirt was washed and ironed for this occasion, Elvan excitedly exclaimed that she wanted Lutfiye to put ringlets in her hair. Hayriye's globular cheekbones protruded, her eyes smiled at her own children, she simply nodded and they carried on eating in silence.
Niyazi reminded her again.
'Anne.'
'Yes oğlum, I heard you.'

The frustrations and dilemmas that ran through his mind were of another kind, he wanted and needed new shoes. He could no longer wear the hand me downs of Elvan's tight moccasins.

(Niyazi, from the bottom, third row far left, holding a catapult)

(Niyazi delivering bread from the bakery)

Chapter 4
July 1964, Tuzla, Cyprus

Leaving Tuzla was going to be arduous for this young married couple, naturally, Sevim grew sentimental about living in the same house Niyazi grew up in. Within five days of conflict and senseless murders, this quaint, pleasant town had ruptured into rubble and ruins. Each crumbling stone was left discarded with the dried, patterned, bloodstains marking lives annihilated through division and patriotism. Last night Niyazi heard that his own primary school was shot at with continuous bullets, it was a warning for parents and children to self-isolate and obey the curfews. Niyazi left the house in the afternoon to buy essentials. He felt the cold tapping of the wind as he walked down the desolate, destitute path of his childhood. Hediye's house was boarded up with corrugated iron, the little well in the garden had been dusted over and the chicken coups were left open as if the neighbour's cat had ravaged each corner and crevice. Tuzla was abandoned, the Ataturk monument was but a fractured wreck of stone. Niyazi tried to keep his head down, if he looked up, this frail and tortured place would leave a heavy hole in his heart, too difficult to bear. His feet scurried faster than his body and he could see the randomly, placed bullet holes that made permanent dents into the concrete walls. Dried, blooded imprints where a pile of massacre shootings were marked on the walls and ground. The intense and stark reality of last night left a cold, callous chill in the air. Approaching his school, the corner of his eye encouraged his head to turn, his eyes to stare and the tears to well as he saw the windows fragmentised into millions of broken, shattered pieces. The centre stage where he use to sing the anthem in the mornings was full of torn textbooks, it was almost as if they wanted to eradicate anything educational or historical that had taken place.

Hasanoğlu had left the UK long before the conflict had started, Niyazi kept in touch with him, and he wanted to follow in his footsteps. Hayriye and

Mustafa had also left and set up a life in South East London. Mustafa was encouraged to leave Tuzla having been let out of prison a little earlier than his sentence. He saw it as an opportunity to set up any business ventures in London and bring the rest of the Osman family with him. Niyazi had no choice but to stay, Sevim was pregnant with twins and she felt helpless in this foreign land. If they had stayed in Istanbul they would not have been thrown into any of this political state of diaspora.

Niyazi, luckily had close friends he knew wouldn't turn their back on him to follow Makarios' orders. Demetrius was one of them. Demetrius and Niyazi grew up in each other's pockets. They were both from two contrasting worlds, two opposite religions, two strikingly opposing languages and politics. Niyazi's Greek was fluent so he could argue his point forward to Demetrius. Both agreed with one another when it came to the subject of Cyprus. They had been living in unison together for many years, why would they separate now? Was it that the orthodox Roman Catholic Church didn't want this? Nothing could obscure their friendship. Despite being told that they were both enemies under Makarios' orders, they both knew nothing would change. Both grew up with divided identities and had to learn to get along, understand one another. Britain's ruling of Cyprus at least comprised friends and cultures to stay together.

Chapter 5
1950, Tuzla Cyprus

A place where animals are fed salt – this was the meaning behind Tuzla, it fell into the mid-section part of Cyprus. A bleached, white, sandy town with random, deserted, little markets and rough, barren farms. Middle-aged men would sit on their cracked, three-legged stalls to sip their broth, boiled, brewed tea whilst others would slam backgammon tabs to the table in a state of confusion. The women would stay in their own household to keep out of the sun. Gender divisions were the norm in this culture.
There was no sense of time in Tuzla, the days and nights blended, the outstretched hours turned into weeks and the lengthened days loitered along lazily like the donkeys on the field.

Hayriye immediately made Demetrius feel welcome into her home, the gentle tapping of her hand to his forehead was ceremonious as he walked into the door and met to her approval, she would heftily pat him and call him son.

Niyazi at this point had left school (under Mustafa's orders) to help in the bakery. He would wake up every morning before the sun would wake up and ride on his bike to the shop to prepare the dough for the koulouri, pilanuva, and helimli. His closest school friend, Suleyman worked with him in the bakery and together they would make the deliveries to each household in Tuzla. Niyazi would cycle down Hamit Bey sokak to give extra loaves to his mother, Hediye, and Demetrius' mother. The bread was the very substance at every meal time but Helimli required a certain amount of patience along with a certain amount of olive oil to be appreciated fully. Helimli was a meal itself and most often Lutfiye would bake it every Sunday.
Hayriye ensured she would put four to five loaves of bread on the table with every evening meal. That evening it was Kolokasi, one of Niyazi's favourites and Hayriye would pride herself in showing Lutfiye how to cook

this taro root vegetable. Kolakasi resembled a turnip but would be stewed and served with artichokes and lemons picked from the garden.

It took Hayriye many years to toil and sweat to perfect her citrus trees. The fragrance of the lemons would linger along Hamit Bey sokak as Niyazi would cycle home.
Demetrius was no stranger to this household, his family was very much the same, poor farmers who learnt how to get by with very little means. Hayriye's table was full of food that afternoon.
'Hadi oglum.' She would feed the whole village if they could fit into her house.
As each member of the Osman family came to sit down one by one together, Demetrius knew how close his ties were with this family. Taylan and Tansel the youngest of the family were Hayriye's favourites whilst Nidai and Niyazi always remained recluse.
Demetrius started the conversation at the dinner table, the customary thank you for the meal.
'Elinize saglik, did you hear Hayriye abla about the riots last night in Nicosia?'
Hayriye was aware of the growth of EOKA since Makarios' popularity; she ignored him as she started to spoon the food into each child's plate, her family responsibilities were far greater than any political problem on the island. Niyazi remained interested and asked 'What happened?' Demetrius turned to Niyazi and Nidai as Hayriye returned to the kitchen.
'I heard that some of the Greek civilians started shooting and rioting in the streets, maybe they're influenced by Makarios.'
Demetrius was interrupted by Hayriye. 'Bu Makarios kim, be?'
Niyazi had told his mother many times over the radio every evening about what was happening on the other side of the Island but it was as if she didn't want to believe that these problems could escalate so soon. This is where her worries began, where would she go? Mustafa always talked about England, his reasons for leaving Cyprus were different. He was not popular anymore in Tuzla- the once distinguished Osman Efendicikoğlu surname which his grandfather prided in was now stained and tainted with the ongoing corrupt situations he landed himself and his family in. Two years in prison was not a light sentence in Cyprus! The infamous hun and row of shops that Mustafa had inherited from his father was once the talk of Tuzla; the little café in the corner was the place every young man would assemble to play cards, drink the local çay and talk about the goings-on in the village. Hamit Bey sokak still had the local bakery that Niyazi and Nidai were supervising but its magnificence and glory had now become dishevelled; this was possibly the ideal time for Mustafa and the family to

leave. Hayriye had no reason to uproot her life and as far as she was concerned there was no logic to any of it. What was there for her in England? Where would they go? Where would they live? Why would she go with him? She would be tied to him once more. She felt so free when he was in prison, now she would be even more tied to him in some unknown place where she didn't understand the language. She suddenly realised this was more serious than she thought, an unknown country, unknown territory, another language, and all her family and friends – what would happen to them? Hediye – what about her? Her pupils widened and her heart was racing, she could feel a flush of panic. Aback with fear; she had to speak to Hediye and find out what she was doing. She remained silent, still and calm as she collected the dinner plates, she felt reposed as she watched Taylan and Tansel dance outside into the garden and play with the sheets on the washing line. Niyazi helped bring the dinner plates into the kitchen and he could see her nervousness in her grey, silvery eyes. Her red, pouting cheeks and sultry forehead showed the hours, months and years she slaved in this hot kitchen to prepare food for her seven children. Her back was turned and Niyazi saw it fit to put his arms around her to console her.

'Anne it's just talk at the moment, it will die down don't worry.'

Hayriye knew what he was doing, she also knew that Niyazi was a worrier like her, she untied her apron string and told Niyazi to look after Taylan and Tansel. 'Where are you going?' He asked.

She took a few Turkish Liras from her Stockings and opened her huge, puffy purse which only ever contained a few Turkish kuruş coins. She replied whilst halfway out the door.

'To Hedi's house, I need to talk to her.'

(Niyazi (far left) working at his father's forge as a blacksmith)

(First row, far right, Niyazi and his friends in Cyprus)

Chapter 6
May 1964, Tuzla. Cyprus

Sevim always felt a temptation to pick the lemons from the tree even though Hayriye forbade it. They had to be fully ripened and soaked under the sun's rays before the juices were squeezed into her stews. She had been in Hamit Bey sokak for a month now and developed an understanding of how each one of Niyazi's family thought. Mustafa had already moved to England with all of the children except Niyazi. Yegane wanted to stay indefinitely as she got married there but the others were still single.
It was 1964 and conflict between Greek and Turkish Cypriots was becoming more intense. Unknown massacres in family homes, people dragged in the dead of night and shot down cold-blooded, people on edge not knowing who to talk to. Who were their friends, enemies, or spies? The British base in Ayios stayed stagnant with British soldiers who were there to keep the peace.

Tonight, Hayriye was cooking molokhia, this was a delicacy Sevim learnt from her and picked up quickly. Molokhia leaves (from a corchorus olitorius plant) was a lemony casserole that she enjoyed cooking and tasting. It was an excuse for her to pick fifteen of the ripest lemons from the tree. Hayriye had taught her everything from picking to preparing with precision. As she was the new gelin in the house, Hayriye wanted to make sure every tradition was passed down properly. She would go into the garden; she had now familiarised herself with the ritual of picking the best and most ripe lemons, she would gently press the lemon's bald belly to feel its juices inside. She would scrape the skin and as soon as she could smell its strong fragrance she knew it was ready for sacrifice.

Sevim felt a sense of gratitude for her new mother-in-law, she felt closer to her than her own mother. Hayriye's harsh, facial exterior was never to be mistaken for her gentle and warm interior. She was sixty-two when she met Sevim and the intricate, infinite, wrinkled paths around her eyes showed the hardships she had. She had aged young and the grey, steel stems of hair that had seeped through, marked years on her own internal imprisonment. Her cruel, scathing world was first marked at the age of thirteen when Mustafa saw it fit to control and dominate every nucleus of her being. He impregnated her for the first fifteen years and left her beaten for the other fifteen.

As they all laid the table that evening, Hayriye brought the huge, clay tureen of molokhia and started to serve the steaming casserole dish. Niyazi broke the silence as he asked his mother.
'Have you packed your things anne? Everything? You know you'll probably not come back for a while - maybe never.'
She nodded as she was ladling the dripping molokhia from the tureen.
'Yes oğlum, don't worry oğlum, you and Sevim need to come as soon as you can. Why aren't you coming with me? You have had your honeymoon here; it's been over two weeks!'
Sevim glanced over to Niyazi and he acknowledged her glance.
'We will anne, I'm taking Sevim to the doctor tomorrow, she's been complaining about this stomach bug for two weeks now.'
Sevim wanted to devour the molokhia like a ravenous animal but her nausea kept coming back.

(Sevim tearing Niyazi's shirts and Niyazi finds them)

Chapter 7
May 1964, Tuzla. Cyprus

Hayriye made her way over to Hedi's house whilst the Muezzin's call was being read. She noticed Hedi placing her praying mat down and dutifully bending her knees. Hediye's praying was more customary than anything else, although Hayriye questioned many things in Islam she would never question them in front of her. As she continued to pray, Hayriye poured two glasses of strong Turkish tea. There was nothing more satisfying for both of them to sit down in the late afternoon sun and sip their tea whilst talking about the rivalries and romance of each member of their family. Hediye this time broke the silence, she walked in with her tespi still counting and praying at the same time.
'Hayros, why have you come earlier today? What's the panic?' She would call her Hayros from time to time, it was a term of endearment. She laughed as she slapped her knee and took a short sip of her tea.
'Did you not hear about the riots last night in Lefkoşa? Niyazi told me, it looks like we will face some hard times ahead Hediye and if it is the case, Mustafa will give a reason to move out of here and go to England- maybe for good.'

She stopped – took another sip and then misplaced the saucer as she put the cup down. They both sat there for what seemed like hours but it was in fact just several minutes for them to watch the hazy sun tire itself out. Hediye knew Hayriye would leave the island and she also knew she didn't have a choice. The silence eventually broke with talk about a local wedding in a few days.
'Will you go Hayriye? You must buy some gold for the bride.' Hediye asked.
Hayriye seemed to ignore the conversation about the bride, the gold, and the wedding, her piercing eyes looked once more at the tired out sun.
'What will I do Hedi? I must go with him but I can't stand him anymore.' Hediye seemed hopeful. 'I heard you can get a divorce in England easily, they say it's fashionable now you know.'
'Fashionable?'
'Hayros, you have endured him up to now, just wait until you get to England and you can divorce him.'
Hayriye knew she was right. 'What will you do Hedi?' She asked but she knew what the answer was.

'You know I will stay here, Hayros with Fuat.' This Ercan name must uphold anything that stands in its way. Hediye was proud of the Ercan legacy and reputation attached to it.

'After all, what can an illiterate person like me do anywhere else, I've not left this island once in my life, where would I go?'

She then went back to slowly sipping her tea in silence. Hayriye nodded her head to show understanding, she was now beginning to contemplate this word divorce. She felt a surge of hope with what Hediye had said. This could actually be a new beginning for her in England. Most of her children spoke English anyway, she would learn too, Niyazi was always a good teacher. At that point, both of them sat on the veranda nodding simultaneously in agreement and searching for the exhausted sun to now slumber down for the day.

This particular day was full of commotion and chaos, the whole Osman family were packing their belongings and preparing to exit to the UK. Hayriye felt she had no choice but to leave. This peaceful, lazy island had become uprooted almost overnight with politics, poison, and punishment and she sensed it day by day. She didn't pack much with her that day, it was so difficult to say her last goodbye like this to everyone she knew. It was too final, too abrupt but she knew it would be difficult for her to come back again, she knew she had to start her life again in London. She had no expectations of what it was like, she knew it would save her and her family from the current situation.

Her suitcase was brimmed with her children's clothes with secretly stashed photos of the family crammed in the sides so that no one could see her, her brother Hussein had already left with his children. She circled the house once more before she closed the heavy, iron door of the kitchen. She was ready to face a change of life…

(From top row left to right. Mustafa, Lutfiye second row Taylan, Hayriye bottom row Tansel)

(Niyazi in Cyprus)

Chapter 8
1938 - 1961 Istanbul, Turkey

One of the reasons why Sevim felt the recognition and respect for Hayriye was because she saw herself in her. Sevim's mother Emine Ibrahimoğlular and family originally came from Safranbolu. Emine moved to Istanbul at the age of seventeen with her brother and aunt Nedime. She moved in with Nedime and her husband Abdullah who was preoccupied with work on most days. He would transport dried products such as hazelnuts, dried figs, almonds and spices from Eminönü the bustling centre to the local markets in Istanbul. Emine fell in love quickly and married. The rest of her family in Safranbolu saw it fit to disown her and her aunt because of her choice of marriage. This was always questioned, did they disapprove of her marriage choice or was she just a little too unorthodox for a fifteen-year-old Turkish girl from the Black Sea region? The day Emine left for Istanbul was the last day she would ever see her mother Kezban again.

Their impoverished lives and lifestyle in Istanbul continued throughout the Second World War. Emine lived in a one-bedroom house in Yedikule, she got married within a year and had Sevim but when Sevim was six months old her father died. Emine was widowed at eighteen and had to go back to the paint factory where she worked almost immediately. Nedime looked after Sevim whilst she worked. Within a year she met Fuat – her second husband and they both worked tirelessly and productively to live a simple and uncomplicated life in Istanbul. Their bungalow was small but they had a huge garden where Emine would show off her love of horticulture and grow her vegetables.

Emine and Fuat lived an unconventional life as a married couple in Istanbul in 1950, many women did not work unless they had to but Emine was never afraid of hard, harsh, industrious work. She wanted to make sure she could put food on the table to feed her now five children, Sevim, Umran, Salih, Türkan and Hamit. Everyone including Sevim accepted and believed that she was Fuat's child, of course, it wasn't something that should be questioned.

One of the most tragic events that affected Emine her whole life was the death of Umran (her second eldest child). Umran was the daughter that was admired the most. She had sun-bleached, blonde hair and the colour of her eyes matched the Bosphorus Sea. Moreover, her movements, posture and gestures had a sense of tranquillity and serenity about them. She was praised at school for being the most intelligent and industrious of the Akdağ family but it ended too abruptly of the summer in 1948.

All three sisters Sevim (ten) Umran (nine) and Türkan (eight) decided to get together with friends after school. Upon seeing a discarded horse cart on top of the hill; they felt intrigued to explore. They were after all just innocent children seeking adventure on a warm, summer day. The Jandarma in those days used huge boulders to place under wheels of carts as there were no brakes in the cart. Everyone decided to get inside the cart; unknowingly two boys from the neighbourhood lifted the boulder and moved it to the side. The cart immediately sped down the hill like a tiny pushchair whose wheels were about to drop off. Sevim pushed Türkan out and threw herself out of the cart in a matter of seconds. Sevim's whole torso thrust forward, she turned to look at Türkan who struggled to get up like a fawn learning to walk for the first time. Then in almost slow motion, she saw the cart hurl about in somersaults with Umran rolling around and out like a delicate butterfly whose wings were being tethered; that's when Sevim's heart sank to the bottom of her abdomen. She not only realised that Umran did not get out, but she was also faced with a lifetime of guilt for not pushing her out first. Umran flopped to the ground and the cart's wheel sunk into her neck. She died instantly. It was from this day onward that Emine had changed, her Umran was gone and part of her had gone with Umran, she was never the same. It was as if Emine's innocence and joy of life had been sucked out of her, placed and sealed in a vacuum capsule for life. Sevim felt she had served a life sentence of guilt for not rescuing her baby sister, that guilt remained raw and fresh in her mind for life.

At dusk, on the same day, her body was buried. Sevim prepared the helva on the hob as she noticed her father signalling the men and women into different rooms for the mevlut to be read. Emine sat in the corner of the living room on her prayer mat, she had been there for two hours since they got back. Her head was covered with a soft, muslin, white veil and she looked like a delicate, fragile vase as she sat still in prayer position. She was not even twenty- five and she had been exposed to another death of a loved one.

At sixteen Sevim had just finished Lise; with no other option but to support her mother and Hamit, she found work in a pharmaceutical laboratory mixing medicine for hospitals in the Beyazit area. She would work there most evenings when her mother and father would come home to look after Hamit, he was five years old and this was the only way they could put a system in place to babysit the youngest child. Sevim found it a struggle to look after Hamit in the day time, at five years old he was notorious in Fatih for causing trouble in the streets with elderly folk outside.

Türkan by this time had just got married to Erhan, a young trader who had obviously mesmerized her into a state of young love with his own dreams of what he could own and make of himself. Suddenly Istanbul woke up and started to prepare itself to become a bustling, centre port of trade, business and money. Erhan had the charm and whimsical behaviour to entrance anyone into his conversation. Salih found work in a newspaper print company in Şişli and moved out almost immediately.
Sevim dreamt of University, she had unreachable dreams but life in Fatih was a vivid reminder of the penniless life she was committed to financially. Her escape, her one way out was obviously Niyazi and Niyazi's one way out was England.

(Sevim far left in Lise with friends)

(Sevim left and aunt Nedime, middle)

(Sevim left and her younger sister Türkan)

(Türkan, Sevim's younger sister marrying Erhan)

(Sevim, in front working in the pharmaceutical laboratory with her sister)

Chapter 9
1963 Turkey, Istanbul and UK, London

It is quite strange and yet surreal how two people who live in two different countries can become pen pals in 1960. Some would claim that Sevim and Niyazi's love was destined but their postal relationship wasn't based on love or passion but more so on trust, companionship, and loyalty.
Sevim had just recovered from a torrent, passionate love affair with Tarik a naval officer.
He would follow her to the tramline every morning when she was going to Beyazit to work. She lapped the compliments whilst holding her handbag and her eyes would glisten when she saw him in his naval uniform. This desire was short lived when his demands that they marry and live with his mother caused Sevim to decline his offer. She was more worthy than this, it was not what she was searching for, a naval officer, uniform, and Tarik appeal was not enough for her.

Niyazi was trying to escape from a formal arranged marriage Mustafa tried to arrange with a local Turkish Cypriot in Tuzla. Niyazi went as far as attending the family ceremony. It was there that Mustafa coaxed him into marrying young; he stamped her foot as a sign sealing the arranged marriage. Months later as wedding plans were being organised he was told that she was infertile and felt obligated to cancel the ceremony. Niyazi wanted children and a family with such a desire, his priority was to be a father to his children that Mustafa never was to him.

Niyazi was moving quite freely between Cyprus and London; many immigrants at the time were shuffling around between countries. The tensions between Greek and Turkish Cypriots were rising each year and many people were told in the village that Britain offered hope and new horizons. For Niyazi it meant economic stability. Many of his friends had already left and it was the perfect time to become independent from his own family, especially Mustafa.

It was in London that he met and became very close friends with a successful lawyer Niyazi Benon whose business was in Knightsbridge, he and his wife Halide were of Turkish origin.
Halide was a talented, portrait artist, she had been asked to paint Queen Elizabeth's portrait, they were well known in the West London community for their established lifestyle. Her exclusive London apartment had huge six, foot tall canvases of horses; her famous painting was "hamam" picturing an image of women washing each other in a hamam.
As an established lawyer, Niyazi would conduct a lot of business in London and Istanbul. He and Halide had an apartment in Istanbul and every so often they would fly over for business and stay to see some of Niyazi's friends who were also lawyers. Niyazi asked his friend whether he knew anyone who wanted to get married and move to England.

One of Niyazi's lawyer friends was Hikmet, Hikmet happened to be married to Meral who was Sevim's closest friend. One evening, they met up and Hikmet put the proposal of being penpals forward to Sevim.
She found the idea romantic and yet practical. She enjoyed writing, this way she had complete command of how slowly she wanted to take everything, it was optimal for her.

That evening she went back to her home in Fatih and used her typewriter to write Niyazi a letter, she was honest and yet quite boastful about her independent lifestyle in Istanbul.
Upon receiving the first typed letter, Niyazi was excited; he felt that a long-distance relationship through letters allowed him to be imaginative about his situation.
In her letters, Sevim would boast about her friends, Istanbul and how beautifully clean it was, she did assume England, London was cleaner.
Niyazi would send post-cards of Trafalgar square, Buckingham Palace and other historical monumental areas explaining how close in vicinity they were of his home in New Cross.

Both of them seemed to compete with one another with their letters. Sevim would describe Florya beach and where she would go on the weekends. Niyazi would show various post-cards of countries he had already been to Italy, France, and Bulgaria. Sevim would laugh every time he wrote to her with the English keyboard, she found some of the misspellings hysterical as the English type writer keyboard had many Turkish letters missing.

Month after month each letter accumulated with an Elle magazine, a pair of the latest silk stockings and occasionally a one-pound note would slip out. Sevim knew that however much she tried to write about Istanbul, her desire and desperation to leave Fatih grew more ardent with each letter. Her life revolved around these two worlds, the world of economic and financial independence and Fatih, the place that would fall into darkness every evening. Fatih was known to be one of the first places to get an electricity cut and the last to have electricity back on. The streets would lie destitute apart from the cockroaches and rats that would scatter the area claiming it theirs. Some evenings, Sevim would come back to a house of darkness and no water, she would find Emine feeding Hamit bread and milk. Her step-father would often work long hours and stay at the café to warm up in the winter days. Sevim only knew a life of struggle like this, she had experienced it as a child growing up and rationing food during the Second World War and she was experiencing it again. Her sister Türkan was fortunate enough to find love, marriage, move out and move on.

Sevim received one package which was heftier than usual. Her smile was brimming as Meral rushed her to open it. It was the latest edition of July's Cosmopolitan, Sevim knew that she could sew and crochet the latest designs using the pictures. As she picked up the magazine from the rim, sterling notes fell like confetti on her lap. Meral started to bombard her with questions. 'Where is this relationship going? What will you do Sevim? Will you marry him? Will you leave your mother and brother in Istanbul here?' Meral's questions were irrelevant, she was as fortunate as every other Istanbul woman who felt that only a man or marriage could save her from financial calamity. Sevim was a cynic with marriage, men and relationships. She was incredibly proud and would not under any circumstance show any man how weak or vulnerable she was. Niyazi however was not like other men (including Tarik). He had a sense of cavalier about him in his courtship and mannerisms. Niyazi was not caught up in controlling women, he wanted to explore life, the world and needed a close friend to travel with him. He admired Sevim's independence, her headstrong mindedness, many other men would be afraid of this assertiveness that she had, but he felt it allowed her to be who she was. Obviously, marriage was to be taken seriously with both of them, it was a contract they were bided to, especially after their previous rendezvous. Niyazi was not looking for a housewife, cleaner or homemaker, he was searching for a lifelong friend to share his wishes, desires and secrets.
Their letters, photos, postcards and personal messages continued for the next three years from England to Turkey via Cyprus.

(Sevim writing to Niyazi whilst they were pen friends)

Chapter 10
June 1964. Tuzla, Cyprus

Tuzla became a dilapidated and hostile place in 1964. Along with other streets, towns, and homes, it got caught up in a tense coil of commotion. The evenings felt long and tedious with curfews and gunshots in the distance. The lemon and fig trees became wrinkled, discoloured, and dry, the sweet and bitter juices were long-drawn and the dust from the shooting became a sickening brown course sheet that covered the ground.
Niyazi could sense when the sudden combustion of gunfire would start late in the evening. What would start off as an eerie, quiet day would submerge into a catastrophic carnage of bodies that piled the streets.

The evenings were the worst, Niyazi dug a well in the garden and placed some concrete slabs around it so they could both use it as a toilet. Late into the evening when the darkness claimed the sky, Sevim would lay awake the whole night trying to put off the inevitable, a trip to the toilet.

Niyazi wanted to show Sevim how to produce and consume the basic necessities whilst they were there. Milking the goats was a little too ambitious, Niyazi would show her how to position the hands on the teat and would gently pat the goat and walk it around the yard so her milk could fill up.

It had been two months since they were there and this honeymoon for Sevim was turning into a much-prolonged vacation, what was worse she was two months pregnant and knew they would be stuck there for what was going to seem like an eternity. Turkish / Greek conflict was constantly flaring up in places around Turkish and Greek towns. There was no television but Niyazi would hear about what was going on. In the neighbouring village, Hamit Koy, Niyazi heard that normal civilians were forced out of their homes onto the streets in the middle of the night whilst their belongings were ransacked, damaged, and stolen.

'Line up and be searched' were the orders and commands given by the "special constables". Niyazi knew it was an offence to carry unlicensed weapons of any kind in Cyprus, he had a sporting rifle that he used for shooting pigeons but these "special constables" were using sporting rifles. He heard about machine guns, pistols, and different types of rifles that were carried around.

The next morning, as both of them headed down to the hospital for Sevim's check-up, Niyazi noticed the streets looked sinister, neglected, and discarded. They spotted the bronze Ataturk statue had been fired at and Makarios billboard photos everywhere. This didn't stop Sevim's excitement but when she was told there were twins that morning she was stupefied.

Apart from her morning sickness, Sevim felt content. She would get a bitter craving in the early mornings and Niyazi would always squeeze a jar full of lemons picked from the garden to get rid of her nausea.

(Sevim and their goat in Tuzla)

Chapter 11
1963 Istanbul, Turkey. UK

In his last letter, Niyazi decided to go to Istanbul to see Sevim, they had both mutually agreed to be married. This was not a trip that he took lightly. The journey took three days and three nights to Sirkeci and Niyazi felt like an excited boy about to receive presents. He would present her with a handmade dowry chest, his life, and a family. The chest was like an overweight brown; grizzly bear made of the most intricately designed and elaborate chestnut wood. The smooth and glazed protruding designs were in the shape of petals and on the front was an enlarged, copper clasp. The chest was put on a different train to arrive in Sirkeci in three days. It must have weighed over a hundred kilos and was packed with every single item you could think of for their honeymoon home.

 He got on the train to Sirkeci with his older sister Lutfiye. From Edirne he made sure he told her what time the train would arrive.
'How will I recognize you?' Sevim asked excitedly.
'My hair is golden blonde and when the train comes into the platform I will peer out of the open window.'

It was crowded in Sirkeci that day. Sirkeci stood like an old elaborate museum in the distance, its orbed pot hole, shaped windows built by the Ottomans became infamous to Sirkeci's architectural system. The gleam on the uneven wooden flooring had not changed since 1888. Each mark and scrape represented the scars of history of every man and woman who walked through Sirkeci and used it as a stopping ground to change their lives. Sirkeci was the only train station in Turkey to have trains going into the European segments of the world. Europe was still a place of palaces where green one-pound notes like golden nuggets would be placed into your hand for free on the entrance. A place where anyone could reach their dreams because it was just a train ride away from Asia. If only it was that simple. Obtaining a visa, an invitation, and an accumulative amount of savings, was just a small portion of the embassy needed. Sevim knew that the place where you were born meant everything to your future and what you made of your life. She had a burning love and passion for Istanbul which she treasured her whole life but it was not the place to have for a future.

The local women huddled to the ground with baggage of over-seaming blankets and scarves. Old wrinkled men crouched to the floor with their wafer-thin tuton cigarettes pinned to their bottom lips. Others sipped their dark brewed çay and scrunched their eyes in the everlasting strong sun.

Aloof, Sevim was standing at the beginning of the platform looking out of place with her tight green pencil skirt and dark shades, she had brought Meral and Necdat for support.
Nothing could be heard apart from the train's roaring shriek as it coughed its way into the platform. Sevim stood suave like a still self-portrait admired by the whole Turkish male population on the platform. The only movement she made was when she withdrew the black leather cigarette holder from her mouth and tilted her mouth at an angle to blow the excess smoke out. The cigarette holder was the first thing she had bought with her monthly salary from the pharmaceutical company, she had placed the rest in an envelope every month to help her mother Emine.

Niyazi bellowed in the distance as soon as he saw Sevim's dark, thick curls. Sevim's figure drifted into long, flowing movements towards him, as Niyazi darted out from one carriage window to another trying to catch up to the first carriage. Sevim was in a state of stupor as she saw a mop of yellow blonde hair flicking in and out of each carriage window until Niyazi made it to the first carriage. Niyazi stepped out with his navy, blue pinned striped suit; he felt acquainted enough to hold her tightly almost immediately. If he had the courage to kiss her he would but Sevim shied away from embarrassment. She was aware that Cyprus was more cosmopolitan than Turkey, the British base in Cyprus had a major influence in terms of how people saw one another and Turkey was more traditional in its courting customs.
Necdat took Niyazi's hand to shake and gave his solemn and brotherly approval. As the introductions were taking place between Meral and Niyazi, Lutfiye sauntered down from the platform in her fox tail wrap and brown suede gloves. She was overdressed for the occasion and felt flustered with the warm change of temperature. Lutfiye was both reserved, formal, and protective when she shook Sevim's hand. She was Hayriye's eldest child but also a huge, protective element in Niyazi's life.
They all left together to a patisserie in Beyoğlu, this was Sevim's favourite past time place. They both spoke about their exchange of letters in greater

depth. Niyazi was spellbound by Sevim's enigmatic, dark, piercing eyes. Sevim enjoyed the attention; she would sometimes flaunter it by swiftly moving her side parting to her left. Her high cheekbones captivated Niyazi as he felt almost flustered with embarrassment at his thin, shapeless legs and protruding, angular bones. Sevim gave a second glance to discover how lean he was. She could see the outlines of his rib cage and felt slightly flustered at her own meaty weight. Had he been starved in Cyprus? She felt slightly awkward that she had been too comfortable with the sterling he had sent. She chuckled when Niyazi ordered his tea with milk, she was slightly confused about how tea could be drunk with milk. Niyazi was oblivious to this as he continued to look and feel mesmerized by her sharp, cryptic eyes that never left his sight. She was a little reserved in showing or expressing any feelings of interest, this did not seem to bother Niyazi in the slightest, and he knew from her letters that she was more pragmatic, and less romantic than he was. Niyazi had been too used to certain ways back in the UK and Cyprus, he enjoyed Istanbul and was looking forward to spending his days here but deep down he missed the village of Tuzla, the peace and quiet…

Niyazi checked in at a hotel opposite Sevim's house in Fatih, they had arranged to go to Sariyer the next day and from there to catch a ferry to Kilyos. She wanted to show him her favourite places, he was well travelled anyway but enjoyed the experience of seeing what she would like to see. They left for Sariyer in the break of dawn so they could enjoy the warm, fresh su borek it was famous for. From there they caught the ferry to Kilyos, renowned for being one of the rawer, natural beaches for Niyazi to discover. They sauntered aimlessly around the tiny pocket corner shops that sold handmade Şile muslin cloth. Niyazi had a fascination with this organic natural cloth, he sympathized with the young, helpless women who sat in the dark corner or a store behind a loom for days to hand weave the material themselves. As he stared fixated at each stitching, he recollected how Hayriye had also worked hard in the fields on her own. He saw the pity in these young women's eyes as they rocked their babies to sleep on their legs whilst using their arms to work the loom.

The sun was strong enough for both to wave their feet in the salty sea. They walked along the sunset dipping their feet into the warm, glistening water. Niyazi spoke heartily about the split world he resided in and Sevim listened intently as she squinted her eyes at the sinking sun. The lazy warmth of that afternoon drew them closer together, although Sevim still kept herself reserved, she couldn't help notice how her eyes gazed at his lips as he spoke about his life back home.

Niyazi knew Sevim had not been to any of the islands of Istanbul and on the few occasions that he had travelled here, he had had some experience of them. Büyük Ada was a pleasant ferry ride away from Eminonu and Niyazi knew it would be a picturesque walk for both to get to know each other more. They took a horse-drawn carriage to the intimate small monastery south of the island, Niyazi asked the local farmer for a key to the arched shaped door. As they walked into the silence of the stoned, shaped dome, they were struck by the serenity it gave them. Their footsteps echoed on the marble flooring as they spiralled around to see the contrasting pictures of Christ and chandeliers hung from the same ceiling. What seemed to be a quaint and rather deserted Orthodox Church was overwhelmed with elaborate, golden, painted altars and pillars.

They walked along the forestry path picking the purple-blue mulberries off the trees. As they headed down towards the harbour, they disclosed their past to one another. Niyazi had an uncanny bond with the church, he wasn't religious but he had an unconditional past and relationship in Cyprus with Greek and Turkish Cypriot friends he had made. He could not hate a race that he grew up with and possibly this became the reason why he would not join the army. Sevim's childhood contrasted with Niyazi's in Istanbul. She had never had a life that was easy or simple, it was consistently a battle for her. At the age of eight, she had to deal with weekly rations to feed her step-siblings. She had always known her purse to be empty, Niyazi was quick to sympathise with her predicament, and he knew that Hayriye would hide money away from Mustafa in several places.

Their afternoons together were endless as they spent most of their time wandering around one area to another. In the Boğazı Strait they would drink gazoz, in Lale Bahce they would drink Ayran, and at Besiktas they shared a plate of mussels. Their warm company was entangled with the closeness and by the end of the evening they enveloped their arms together. By the fourth day, the dowry had arrived in the huge chest Niyazi had bought. The chest was delivered to her house and Niyazi was careful with what and how he had packed everything. He had bought Sevim the latest and most modern slow cooker that was available in the UK. Sevim was aghast as Niyazi opened the lid to the slow cooker with the clasp.

'You mean I don't have to stand over and stir?' She asked in the most gullible way. He laughed as he told her. 'You are free to do what you want, it will cook itself.' The slow cooker itself must have weighed ten kilos, the lid was as heavy as the base.

Sevim had given him her waist, hip, and bust measurements, so the chest was also packed with gingham dresses, culottes, and evening wear. In the corner, Sevim noticed a white lace collar, she uncovered the blankets to find a wedding dress, and he had got it tailor-made, measured for her. The bodice was tight, Sevim's waist was narrow, and she knew the fitting was accurate.

They both got registered in a tiny register office in Fatih later that week in Saricahane. It was a private venue, a circle of six friends had arrived and Lutfiye to witness the registration, Niyazi paid children sweets to come in and observe the ceremony.

They rented a home in Beyazit for a month before they got the ferry to Cyprus. Niyazi had to go back to see Yegane before they could start their life in the UK, she was the only remaining sister to stay there and was going to stay there permanently.

This was to be their honeymoon and place of prison for the next year to come...

(Sevim and Niyazi getting married in Istanbul)

(Sevim visiting Buyuk Ada in Istanbul)

Chapter 12
April 1964 Tuzla, Cyprus

Arrival after the honeymoon.

They had arrived in Tuzla and Sevim stopped to question where she was and what she had done. It was incredibly smaller than she imagined, it looked like a primitive medieval village.
'Mind you' she said 'I have lived in Istanbul my whole life.'
'We won't be here for long, I'm just checking on the house and Yegane, we will be out of here in no time and leave for London.' He said comfortingly, he sensed she did not want to be here but he had no choice but to look after some issues with the house and shops that they had left to workers. Sevim felt a sense of relief although she didn't want to tell him that.

She spent the first few days asking Niyazi endless questions.
'Where is the toilet? How do you use the toilet flush? How do you use the shower? What is the funnel for in the shower? Niyazi smirked with every naive question but was incredibly patient and tolerant with Sevim. Sevim felt abhorrence but tried to shake this off with sarcasm, Yegane could see she was a city woman. She would often make similar sarcastic comments about her upbringing in Istanbul and how much of an alien she must have felt in a small village like Tuzla.
'The funnel is the showerhead', Yegane pointed out to Sevim, this was Niyazi's immaculate invention of the garden hose and funnel to make a shower. She then laughed to show Sevim how much more she knew about her own brother.
'He's always making something out of nothing, you see this here Avery where we keep our pigeons and doves.' She pointed at the huge ten-foot avery made of mesh and wood. She walked over to find pigeons on one side cooing and doves on the other, the male doves were strutting their heads up and down chasing the females.

'It's the mating season.' Yegane said. Sevim was a lot more inquisitive now. 'How can you tell?' She asked.

'They play this chasing game, the male dove here, see what he is doing, he is bobbing his head up and down to dance and impress the female.' As she pointed to the bigger and broader dove, she carried on explaining.

Sevim was entranced to watch couples of doves dancing around each other, it looked like a romantic sequenced dance. Yegane was right, she was learning more about him by being in Tuzla, and he never mentioned his love for animals.

Yegane picked up the pigeon eggs and smiled at Sevim. 'He keeps the pigeons because of their eggs, he cooks with them.' She added.

Sevim was confused; she had never eaten pigeon eggs before. Whilst standing in utter disbelief, Niyazi opened the avery door to perch two doves on his hands. He asked her to stroke them and as she did, he added, the meat is nice too, 'pigeon meat, with lots of salça and potatoes.' He started to smack his lips and grinned at Sevim's shocked face. Sevim was addicted to his child-like grin and dimpled chin, there was a sense of innocence and gullibility about it. She smiled as if she could appreciate his sense of humour but felt bemused by it at the same time. She knew she could not make any comparisons between Istanbul and Tuzla, she also knew there were many facets to Niyazi's life she had to adapt to.

A feeling of appreciation came to her each time she thought about him and his upbringing. He was the middle child brought up in a large family and left discarded to find his own way in the world. He grew up in the dry, fading fields and became citified in the wild, concrete, urban streets of London where the grey clouds wept all day long.

Chapter 13
1960 London, Istanbul and Tuzla

Niyazi mastered the trip from London to Istanbul where he would spend just a few days at a time cruising around the palaces, mosque, and bazaars, appreciating the colossal, historical, sultan figures and their lavished lifestyle. Niyazi never understood the stares and gazes he got from the locals in Sultan Ahmet, he wondered whether his suit attire spotlighted him as a western tourist. His hair was the colour of cornfields and his eyes were pearly, ash grey, not the usual look of a Middle Eastern man. In London he looked like a Londoner, dressed like a Londoner but here in the heart of Istanbul's streets and markets, only diplomats came over in their suits.

In 1960 Mustafa sold parts of his hun in Tuzla and bought property in London. Everyone felt a sigh of relief that they could move out of the area and have a more prosperous life. Hayriye felt most satisfied with this decision. She knew that she never had to feel a feeling of shame again, whenever anyone asked where Mustafa was and when he would be coming home. She also knew that she would not see Hediye again, those soft eyes, that good-natured face, that endless smile, and her tiny pointed chin.

Moving into the seedy part of South East London was a far cry from the wild, blue, azure sun and the sunburnt fields of Tuzla, Niyazi got accustomed to Deptford, the fish market, and the strange mixture of cultures. Deptford had a bizarre mix of Afro- Caribbean, Windrush minorities and Turkish, Cypriot communities compiled together. It was as if someone hand randomly picked these two islands and placed them together. They couldn't have been so different yet Niyazi felt many similarities between Deptford and Tuzla. Two different cultures, languages, and religions living together. Saturday afternoons in Deptford High Street was the focal point for him. There would be stalls strewn across the walk full of homemade Jamaican patties and jerk chicken whilst on the other side he would find sesame and aniseed bread with helim cheese made in London.

He would have flashbacks of when he would cycle into Lefkosa and would converse from Turkish to Greek. The younger generation like himself had adapted to three languages well. They would use their bilingualism to flirt with the girls and English for business. Niyazi's generation had benefitted the most from the current situation in Cyprus. The British army still had control over Cyprus until 1960 and many schools taught English from an early age. When Cyprus gained its independence, some British Army bases were built in Cyprus, and Niyazi benefitted from this. He would often buy British cigarettes off the soldiers and trade them for a higher price in the market. British cigarettes like Dunhill International were hard to come by, and most of the trading was done in English. He would travel back to London for a few months, buy a return ticket and travel around Europe and Turkey. This was his most burning desire, to travel, see the world, and broaden his horizons whilst he could. He delighted himself in buying souvenirs wherever he went. From Dolmabahçe he picked up an old-fashioned red velvet fez. From the Büyük Çarşı he picked up an unused nargile, and from Topkapi, he haggled over an ivory Sultan head smoking pipe. This was his most treasured piece, these kind of pipes were made specifically from ivory because it enhanced the distinct tobacco smell. Niyazi's favourite past time was to light this pipe every Sunday in the afternoon, he wasn't a big smoker at all but he enjoyed smoking his pipe. Quite often his close friend, Niyazi Benon would come over and they would smoke their pipes together.

In Deptford, he started working in the local Deptford café to save up some money to travel. His yearning, to go back to Istanbul frequently was a burning desire since his childhood and read about Constantinople at school. The work at the café was simple and he used it as an opportunity to understand the way of British culture. Once he had earned enough savings; his first train ticket was to Italy. He travelled through Verona, Venice, then down South to the Vatican into Naples. He was in awe of the amphitheatres and the way they had been constructed during the imperial days. He enjoyed his own company and would peruse in his own time around the quaint Italian vineyards, cobbled paths and whitewashed terraced houses. He delighted himself in reading up on the small towns and their historical past. He bought postcards for every city he travelled to and wrote small diary entries so he could saviour the moments of being there. Whilst Niyazi was working at the café in Deptford he invested in an expensive Nikon camera that he knew he could use on his travels. He would spend a huge part of his morning looking into his camera to get the perspective, light and frame accurate and right. Each snapshot of every monumental building was thought with definitude and a curious eye, these were his treasures when he returned, his black and white photos, and a mind stored of the routes he memorised on a map.

Chapter 14
Cyprus, Tuzla May 1964

Sevim's pregnancy was the deciding factor for staying in Cyprus. Niyazi knew that it would be problematic to get on a ship and train to England in that condition, he knew many doctors in Tuzla therefore it seemed the most logical decision to make. Moreover, tensions were rising now between the Greek and Turkish civilians, curfews were being introduced and they felt restricted to stay in their home in Tuzla until a pact was drawn up. Makarios had been newly elected as the president of the republic, and many of Niyazi's friends were fearing the worst. Niyazi left Sevim at home one evening as he went to the local çay house to speak to his friends. He knew this would be the last time he would be able to meet up with his Greek friends and talk freely, Tuzla became a ticking, wired bomb that would explode into tiny fragments everywhere.

As Niyazi walked into the çay house, a few of his Turkish Cypriot friends Yalçın and Timor were already sipping tea and watching the local news. This place was not the same as it was before. Niyazi and the whole family had been scorned ever since Mustafa was let out of prison, the café not only looked bare but everyone sat and stared as if they were solitary, motionless figurines greeting every person at a funeral pyre.

The tall, lanky tea man poured Niyazi's black tea and Niyazi looked around at what other people were doing, they were waiting for the evening news to be broadcasted from a tiny black and white TV box. Niyazi asked hastily
'Where's Demetrius?'
'Did you not hear abi, he was sent early morning yesterday to the military.'

Niyazi was in shock – neither Demetrius nor his family told him. He wondered, was it to keep him safe? Niyazi also knew that military service was lengthened to eighteen months, it would be a blessing if he saw him at all. So he was now legally on the other side, his enemy. They had grown up like brothers, closer than his actual brother, and now they had to act like enemies, worse to shoot the enemy down.

Every evening Niyazi would watch the news to listen to the changes that had taken place, he was on edge about staying in Cyprus, he should have gone to England with Sevim after two weeks but how was he to know that this fraction would escalate. The television was turned on but what Niyazi was not expecting was the Greek national anthem played for the first two minutes.

'What's this?' he said angrily slamming his tea glass down on the table.

Yalçın spoke calmly, 'this is common practice now Niyazi bey, there's no point in being annoyed.'

Niyazi was aware of the changes. Last week he noticed that the road signs had changed to Greek Cyrillic with some English translation in the tourist hot spots. The news was spoken in Greek, and with a brief speech given by Macarios, there were news items about fresh weapons imported by the Greeks to Cyprus. Niyazi's skin was on edge. He knew there was an urgency to leave now with Sevim but she had to give birth in Cyprus, they couldn't leave with her four months pregnant. She found it impossible to walk anywhere longer than a mile before her bladder would burst.

Fuat ran inside the café panting and holding his chest, 'Niyazi abi,' he shrieked.

'There's smoke appearing from your house, I can see it and smell it. Isn't Sevim inside there?'

At that moment Niyazi sprinted across the road, he noticed the lights weren't on and banged on the door, he fidgeted with his keys and burst in. Sevim was lying on the couch sleeping whilst a pot in the kitchen had been set alight with two huge bulging chicken legs sticking out in the most undignified way. Niyazi nudged Sevim and started to panic.

'Sevim, Sevim…' Sevim came to but felt flustered and hot.

'What is it Niyazi?'

She scanned the living room and saw the smoke, a delayed reaction caused her to cough uncontrollably as she stood up to lift herself to the exit. Sevim knew what had happened, at four months pregnant her body clock was tired and she was having uncontrollable naps, she left the pot on the stove to burn.

Fuat assisted Sevim into their house with Hediye for the evening until the smoke had gone away, there was a curfew, and they could not be out of their own home. Hediye was pleased to see them and made the guest room up for them to sleep. Throughout the night they stayed up to hear the shooting in the neighbouring villages. Hediye made dorma for them and they talked about Hayriye. Hediye rocked her hands back and forth to show her disbelief at what was happening around her.

Soon after she crept into her bedroom and came back with a paisley, beige coloured veil and beads.

'Take this' she said.

She opened out Sevim's palm and placed the veil into her hand.

'Give this to my close friend, I have no use for it here. She always liked this veil. A friend of mine bought it for me when she came back from Mecca. Niyazi took Hediye's hand, kissed it, and then placed it to his forehead. It was a gracious gift anyone could give, and Hediye always knew how to be gracious. Hediye looked at Sevim's bump and asked 'how many months are you now my daughter?'

Sevim was delighted to talk about her pregnancy now.

'Four Hediye teyse, we're expecting twins.'

Hediye's smile beamed like a glazed ray.

'Do you know the sex of the babies?'

Sevim was able to confirm this as she had had her first examination a couple of weeks ago.

'Yes one is a boy, one is a girl.' Hediye beckoned her over to sit next to her and stroked her hair.

'Your mother in law will be overjoyed.' She exclaimed and continued to stroke her hair.

Chapter 15
Tuzla June 1964

Sevim flew out of the house to catch up with Niyazi amidst the showering air raids. Six months pregnant, her shapely, voluptuous figure had a prominent curvature that she could not conceal. Niyazi found it difficult to contain any excitement today as they were going to have another check-up and she knew both babies were healthy, her hunger for food turned into desperation.

Niyazi's close friend, Adnan was standing in front of a 1960 blood, red, American corvette that he had bought from one of the bases. Slim and lanky, Adnan had always admired Niyazi, he was the older, trustworthy brother he never had. They met each time Adnan would rush to the bakery after work. He revelled in his jokes and listened intently to the historical stories about Ataturk's attacks. For Niyazi, Adnan was a calming tonic during the times his father was in prison. Niyazi was left to pick up pieces of the family bakery business instantaneously and educate himself too.

Adnan's sandy coloured T-shirt looked unkempt and worn. Bought from the American store on the Greek side; he had a fascination with anything foreign. The American base was temporarily built next to the British, he had a desire to learn about the American culture. Turkish and Greek Cypriots had to stay on their own sides since Macarios' declarations to keep them apart. The British base was placed in Lefkosa since the British had retreated leaving Turks and Greeks to settle this island on their own. As neither side could settle anything democratically the British army was asked to come back. Temporarily, a tiny, narrow side street was set up to stop people from walking or driving from one side to another. What began with a small unit of ten soldiers grew to become three units, they stayed there for longer than thirty years.

Adnan pinched the cigarette with his fingers to put it out and flicked the bud to the floor like it was a speck of dirt. This ten-minute drive turned into an hour, slow procession. Adnan wasn't caught up in traffic, there were Greek Cypriot civilians with rifles crawling the streets and neighbourhoods to find any Turkish Cypriot guilty of a crime. They came to a police check stop, Niyazi handed his and Sevim's passport over. The British soldiers thought they were here for a sunshine vacation. No one would have anticipated that this undersized island where two cultures entwined could be so apart.

The soldier gave a fleeting glance at the passports and nonchalantly moved his hand to show pass. It was incredibly easy to go to the other side, it always had been but, in the last few years since Macarios' leadership, everyone on the island made their way to be separated from one another. Sevim didn't notice much of a difference between these two polar sides, apart from the black wooden crosses left stagnating above the Orthodox Church.
Niyazi however had lost touch with many of his Greek friends, they were either forced to become enemies or closer friends stopped talking to him to protect his identity and safety.
The sun-baked, gritty streets were emptier than usual and both of them knew that some kind of shooting must have happened the night before.
As they both walked into the hospital, Niyazi noticed the corridors were white, void sheets, and the smell of sanitation rose into the air. At that moment, Adnan noticed a small group of Greek civilians circling the area outside the hospital and whistled at Niyazi to gain his attention.
'Entáxei adelfós.' This was Adnan's signal in Greek to say it's ok, it was a warning to Niyazi and he understood.
Niyazi turned around and replied with the same meaning, 'Entaxei' to show his agreement. As he did so, he looked at the civilians straight into their eyes and nodded simultaneously in recognition whilst he called out ' Chairete'.
 Their Greek pronunciation was as perfect as their Turkish, this was the norm for Turkish and Greek Cypriots who were growing up here, and they were integrated within both communities without any problems at all. The local cafes had a mixture of two spoken languages, Greek and Turkish. Cypriot children would hold hands whilst walking to school together, and there were mixed cultural marriages. This was all part of the norm,

acceptance and respect of each other's identity. Niyazi even had a secret rendezvous with a Greek girl in the Tuzla neighbourhood, she fell pregnant by Niyazi quickly and he tried to be honourable by asking for her hand in marriage. Her father, angered by the pregnancy, shooed him away warning him never to meet up with his daughter again. To this day, Niyazi never knew whether she gave birth to his child, her father was quick enough to give her an arranged marriage. These were lost and forgotten days to Niyazi as he looked lovingly at Sevim and her six-month bump, how could he fathom now being with a Greek woman amidst this war zone.

Walking into Famagusta Hospital, nothing had changed, there was still a mixture of Turkish and Greek Cypriot nurses working there. Niyazi asked for the specific midwife who had been looking after Sevim.
The receptionist smiled at Sevim and then their Turkish communication broke with a handshake.
'Welcome', she glared at Sevim's bump, 'You must be having twins!' She said. Sevim was shocked.
'How do you know, she asked?'
The receptionist smiled, took their documents, and showed them to the ultrasound room. Sevim was greeted by the midwife Maria and sat upon the seat waiting to be looked at. Maria was more formal than any nurse Sevim had met, she squeezed the cold gel that fell on to Sevim bulging belly and started rolling this ancient mechanism around.
She started nodding her head and repeating the words 'Naí.'
Sevim looked up at Niyazi.
'O ne demek?' she asked.
It's okay, everything is okay Sevim, and he clutched her hands for reassurance.
The nurse continued rolling the mechanism around, she stared at Sevim into her eyes and asked 'did you know you were having twins? One is a boy the other is a girl?'
'Yes, yes.' Sevim nodded, then the nurse looked up at Niyazi and started to giggle, Sevim was bemused. The nurse laughed as she spoke.
'Seems like the boy is a lot hungrier than the girl, he's a little heavier.'
The nurse cleaned the gel off Sevim's belly and placed a cloth over her as a signal to cover up and get dressed. As Sevim walked behind the screen, the nurse grabbed Niyazi's arm and asked him if his wife was Turkish.
'Yes he replied, isn't it obvious?'
Then you must be careful. These are dangerous times Niyazi bey, we are here today and not tomorrow. Don't you see how empty this hospital is? Have you and your wife not stopped to ask why?' She whispered.

Sevim came out of the screen unaware of their conversation and smiled at the nurse to suggest her gratitude.

As Niyazi walked out of the hospital door; Adnan caught his arm and pulled him to one side.
'Did you realise that there aren't any patients here especially Turkish Cypriot ones Niyazi abi?'
Niyazi nodded in silence to Adnan's questions but this was not the place or time to start questioning why people weren't admitting themselves into the hospital. He turned to call Sevim and got straight into the car. Niyazi could tell Adnan was getting nervous the minute he lit another cigarette and threw the used packet in the glove compartment. Niyazi tried to calm him down.
'It's me and Sevim who are having a baby, calm down a little and drive carefully.' He gently replied. Adnan shuffled his shoulders forward and stayed focussed on the road.
Anyway' he broke out in mid-conversation, 'there was a scuffle here last night, and two Turkish Cypriots were shot by the Greek "special constables" for not showing their identity cards. Sevim almost instantly felt nervous, you could see it in her dismissive look.
'Did they die?' Niyazi asked.
Adnan didn't reply, the answer was obvious. The identity cards and having them around you was an excuse to be shot, everything was an excuse to be shot because the real reason was who you are and where you come from matters now. Niyazi was confused about these kinds of atrocious shootings and killings. They became a norm to him, he still didn't understand why the hospital was empty. It was infamous for having the most up to date equipment, many of the British forces' wives gave birth there, that is why he chose it and Sevim approved. Perhaps it took many years for all of this mess to be uncovered.

Chapter 16
June 1964, London

Below the subterranean depths of the tearful, meagre sky lay the vivacious market streets of Deptford where the boom boxes of Reggae vibrations were heard from one street to another. This was where Mustafa had taken Hayriye and all of his children, out of the raw, rural, rusticity of Tuzla into the throbbing, thumping, assorted crowds that walked from one direction to nowhere. This region of London was known for the overcrowded community of the Turkish Cypriot minorities. Having sold some of his businesses, Mustafa bought an old town house in the heart of Deptford where the whole family stayed and lived.

Niyazi's intention to come back was purely to prepare everything for Sevim and his new, young babies. He had reservations about leaving Sevim in Tuzla but he reassured her it would not be for more than a week and Hediye would look after her.

Niyazi knew exactly what he wanted to do whilst he was in London. He had made an appointment with the solicitor for a name change, from Efendecikoğlu to Işık. Sevim had insisted on changing the surname, Efendecikoğlu did not suit her and she always found it old fashioned. For Niyazi the reasons were different, it was to discard the chains of violence and control for many years. Changing his surname meant emancipation.

Sevim liked the surname Işık, during her younger years when she was working in Istanbul. She would spend much of her time going to the cinema to watch her favourite films of a young, charismatic actor Ayhan Işık. To say she had a crush was an understatement, she was more than willing to ask Niyazi to adopt this new surname and he was so encapsulated by her, he would accept it.

Niyazi wanted to address all of these legalities to set up a new life in London for him and Sevim but when Mustafa found out what he was doing, he was enraged.
'How dare you dispose of the great Efendecikoğlu surname son, it's generations of our past and roots!' Mustafa declared in front of everyone. Throughout Niyazi's life he was never able to voice his opinion to his own father, he feared his hand too much but a sense of urgency came within his own voice when he was there.
"Baba, I have changed it for many reasons." He spoke with his new acclaimed confidence.
 Niyazi's voice was composed, he didn't want to go into any details about how everything had changed in Cyprus, Mustafa had been sheltered both in Prison and when coming to the UK. Mustafa's eyes showed a blood, red gaze of anger when he heard Niyazi. For him, it was dismissive, dishonourable, and discreditable. If Mustafa knew Sevim came up with the idea of a name change, he would have been even more enraged. To think that a woman, from Istanbul, spoilt and capricious could change a surname that had a centurial, legacy in Cyprus. Mustafa's father and uncle were known for their extraordinary bravery in the First World War. They were applauded by the locals when they arrived back to Lefkoşa. Mustafa's innovative, business skills enabled him to haggle on price for the plot of land in Tuzla, this was the place he had built his house, hun and the shops around it. His overbearing, domination filtered through to his treatment of and towards women. Mustafa knew no different than to batter and clobber Hayriye when he was a little drunk or a little tired. Hayriye had been pushed down the stairs in Tuzla on one occasion and miscarried twins on another as a result of his heavy, brutal fist. She had to deal with the late nights he would come home and force himself into her and the absences of his illegal, sordid behaviour that was always unspoken.

Mustafa finally spoke to Niyazi when he came back from the solicitor. When Niyazi walked in with the paper work in his hands; he saw everyone sitting down as if they were in a waiting room. Hayriye broke the silence by pulling him into the kitchen.

'What's happening annecim, why is everyone sitting here in silence?' he asked in a concerned tone. She placed the tea in his hands and watched him look around at everyone cautiously.

As you well know I have been organising my assets from Cyprus to be sent over and placed into the banks here. The deafening silence casted a shadow around the room. Gradually everyone's face rose as soon as they heard the word inheritance. Mustafa had decided to use his bullying tactics to leave nothing to Niyazi as he had disobeyed his orders, listened to a Turkish woman and changed his surname. All of Mustafa's savings and earnings had gone to the younger sibling. Niyazi didn't feel deterred by any of this, he had made his decision and respected Sevim's wishes. In actual fact Niyazi was determined to live his life opposite to how Mustafa led his. Mustafa had become an insignificant non entity in his life and he had just proven it by doing this.

Chapter 17
August 1964, Tuzla

The sweltering heat had long past that year of 1964, and Sevim's walrus weight had started to bare her down like two large watermelons. Late in the evenings, she would begin to sense the two alien, little bodies struggling to turn and poke about. Sometimes as she lay there, she could see fingers darting at her skin as if to knock and get her attention. Sevim at this point was able to decipher the two babies apart, the smaller one seemed to be a lot more unconfident in her movements. She wouldn't raise her hands so much for attention, but the bigger seemed more in control of their black hole dominion. Sevim felt he would push her aside at times to get attention. She would feel tired instantly and constantly, she would lay her head to sleep at the most random times of the day whilst these movements attached to the placenta would take over. Over the course of the months, she felt that the house in Tuzla was her haven since the outside world became a corrupt and decrepit, foreign hostile place. It was once Niyazi's homeland, but all the innocence and tranquillity had been sucked out of it.

As Sevim was hauling herself to the kitchen, she gave a gentle pat on Niyazi's shoulder to show she was awake. Niyazi had been cooking now for the last month. The lemons were still ripe in the garden to make sweet lemonade, and Sevim felt that excitement every day that she could still enjoy sweet, fresh lemonade in the mornings.

Momentarily there was a succession of knocks on the door, Niyazi knew it was Adnan.

'Come in my friend, I've brewed some fresh tea.' Sevim knew why Adnan came over so often. Their friendship group outside the house had diminished, they could no longer go out in the evenings, and Adnan was the only trustworthy friend who knew about their escape. Every month further into Sevim's pregnancy was another month further into the hostility, shooting, fighting, and deaths.

Adnan's embarrassment was still evident as he shook Sevim's hand without looking at her. Sevim always found it difficult to understand the way Cypriots greeted one another, she was always comparing life in Istanbul to Tuzla. Niyazi just ignored Sevim's comments and comparisons, Adnan would nod his head in sympathy and look at her with curiosity. Sevim's voluptuous, beauty radiated even in pregnancy. Her jet, black hair was lustrous to any onlooker. Her eyes brows, long, dark, fierce branches that could sheathe any man's wondrous desires and her wide, onyx eyes would mesmerize anyone who dared to peer her way. Seven months in Tuzla and she was still talked about, it was obvious that Sevim was not from Cyprus at all.

Adnan started to quiz Niyazi about his and Sevim's passports. He knew that escaping and leaving Cyprus was going to be futile but if they did not leave as soon as they could, their town would be next. Niyazi had dual citizenship, he had a British and Turkish / Cypriot passport. When Cyprus was under British rule, it was straight forward for any Cypriot to obtain a British passport. Niyazi would use his British passport whenever he wanted to go to the Greek border and the Greek Cypriots would do the same.

'My passport is not the problem Adnan' Niyazi spoke as he stirred his tea. 'It's Sevim's, she has just a Turkish passport. Makarios has administered a new law now that no Turk or Cypriot Turk can enter the Greek border. This is to avoid any more deaths.' Niyazi added hastily.

'So' Adnan asked, 'how will she leave?'

I'll be honest and say that we got married in Istanbul and came here before the problems began' he continued, 'they might be sympathetic or not. Everything is up in the air at the moment. People get shot now for everything.' He added.

Sevim burst midway into the conversation to state her opinion. 'They should be grateful I want to leave this tiny island, what am I supposed to do here?' she continued.

Part of the plan was that Adnan would sneak Sevim and Niyazi across to the border and from there they would get a ferry across to Italy.

Whilst Niyazi was in London he also put a deposit on a small house in Deptford, so he had established and set everything up. Adnan noticed Sevim place her hands on her belly and decided to change the subject to ease any worry amongst them.

'Have you decided any names yet?' He asked. Before Sevim could answer, Niyazi interrupted.

'I want to call my daughter Hayriye and my son Selcuk.' Adnan was both impressed and proud of what Niyazi said. His love for his mother was so powerful that he wanted to name his daughter after her. He obviously knew Sevim wanted to decide on a name but she was willing to accept this. Adnan turned to Sevim;

'Is that what you want too?' he added to which Sevim nodded gaily and carried on pouring the golden and black Turkish tea.

'Don't worry I will name the next one.' She added.

Chapter 18
Tuzla 1964 Larnaca Hospital

Christmas in Cyprus was a bizarre time, British Soldiers were trying to celebrate the festive time any way they could on the Greek, Catholic side, on the Muslim side it was a typical working day. Christmas had no significance for Niyazi and every other Turkish Cypriot but he would often get himself into a festive spirit and drink with his Greek Cypriot friends. He had a degree of respect and understanding for the way they followed their faith and celebrated it, this stemmed from the way people lived and got on. Geographically, Cyprus was what made the generation what it was and perhaps moulded Niyazi to be the human being that he was.

On 28th December Sevim felt an unusual pain different from the stretch mark pains she had been experiencing, this felt like small contraction pains. She was predicted January 1st as the date that these babies were due, it was four days early. Niyazi asked 'can you walk Sevim?' Sevim could barely hold herself up; every time she took a heavy step, she would feel a surging, knife pain in her abdomen. She would stagger, she would crawl, she would do everything but walk, so Niyazi flagged a taxi instantly and asked for Larnaca Hospital. For Sevim it felt like the longest fifteen minutes of her life, she felt nervous for these babies. Was it the stress that made them come early she asked herself.

They quickly put her in a wheel chair and wheeled her through the corridors of the hospital. Sevim's contractions were coming every seven minutes and with each contraction a wave of piercing pain would render through her as if a foreign spirit had entered and exited her body. Niyazi clenched her hands and looked into those wild, dark eyes, nothing was going to calm or help her at that moment. The doctor spoke to Niyazi almost ignoring Sevim, he explained that they would have to conduct a caesarean as she wasn't fully dilated and both babies were trying to push through. The nurses beside her spoke in Turkish and they were trying to calm her down. Niyazi told her they would give her a general anaesthetic, he had signed the papers for consent and before Sevim could fathom what was happening she closed her eyes and went to sleep.

Chapter 19
Larnaca Hospital, Cyprus

She stirred a little as she was coming round and could feel herself wetting her dry, crusted lips, and then it instantly dawned on her. Her babies – alive – dead? She looked at her belly, at first she was confused, had she given birth? Then the traumatic realisation she had had a caesarean caused her to sink her head back into the pillow. She didn't feel any pain and knew the medication was working. It was as if she was placed in a white, coffin box with a curtain pulled around surrounding her whole body. She heard a couple of nurses in the background whispering in Greek and wondered if they had anticipated she was awake. She recognised from the gentle patting of footsteps that the doctor was walking away, and the same welcoming nurse pulled back the white, sanitised curtains abruptly as if catching Sevim out. 'Good Afternoon Sevim, your babies were born each at four pounds this afternoon.' She spoke as she pushed the trolley bed into the ward. Abruptly, she started to swirl the trolley bed through the corridor leaving Sevim almost dazed.

The nurse continued 'they are both healthy except the boy has little jaundice and fever but that's natural.' Sevim's drowsy head jolted upright when she heard jaundice and fever.

'Don't be alarmed.' The nurse continued 'most babies are born with jaundice; we have wrapped a hot water bottle and placed it near him so he is not cold.'

Alert and confused, Sevim knew that many babies got jaundice when they were first born but she did not understand why a hot water bottle was needed. She cut the nurse's conversation short with a simple request.

'Can I see them please?'

So for the first and last time that day, Sevim was reunited with both her babies together. Both Selcuk and Hayriye looked tiny and malnourished. She held Selcuk tightly before they insisted on taking him back because of his jaundice. His little yellow body looked helpless; his eyes were constantly shut as if in an endless dream. She could see the dull, yellow, thin layer covering his body and lay him back down for fear of waking him. His strong fingers clenched Sevim's thumb, and she could see him drifting in and out of a dream.

Then her attention turned to Hayriye, she looked smaller and more fragile, her hair was silky, soft and straightened every time Sevim stroked her. She could sit and watch them both the whole day and recognize something different about them every minute. It was as if they were evolving every second. Niyazi was in the corner of the room writing in his diary, at first point it would seem that he looked composed, calm, and collect in his emotions, but his head was down as he wrote the time, day, and details of his children's birth. No one had ever made him feel this honoured and yet these two helpless, warm babies sleeping side to side did just that.

However, the next morning all of this had changed when the nurse walked in. Sevim was barely awake, she was still trying to adjust to the sleepless night and broken sleep she had, the nurses did not wake her, and the babies were bottled fed that night so that Sevim could recover. The nurse's face was solemn and she found it difficult to look at Sevim's eyes. 'Over the course of the night', she said 'the hot water bottle leaked and it scorned Selcuk alive. I'm sorry' she spoke in a hushed voice and then almost in surprise she spoke in Turkish 'başınız sağolsun'.

That was the first she had heard her speak in Turkish. With a cruel and harsh reality that surrounded her in Tuzla, she saw the empathy in the nurse's heart. Sevim did not know how to perceive those weeks in the hospital, she felt as if she over thought Selcuk's death by constantly asking herself questions. Was it destiny that Hayriye should have survived this ordeal? She was lying next to him when he had the hot water bottle over him the whole night.

They both felt stripped of their dignity as they walked to the graveyard at the back of the hospital to pay their last respects, Hayriye was sleeping in Sevim's arms.
The sky opened up its wound that day red and raw to gulp a helpless baby and both Niyazi and Sevim consented to this with no questions asked. The burial did not take longer than ten minutes. They stood there in silence as if they did not know what to say to one another. No hoca was called, it was too dangerous for them to have a Muslim ceremony, Niyazi didn't want to be traced in the last few months he was going to stay here. The priest gave a simple prayer, and Niyazi tipped him as they started to walk back. Clutching Niyazi's arm back, Sevim quizzed him.
'Where are you going Niyazi?' Niyazi looked as if he ignored her as he carried on walking but he muttered under his breath, 'it's over!'
Sevim had only one photograph of these two babies together, but she put it amongst the pile of stay for Yegane to keep safe along with other belongings. Yegane was the only person to have one copy of the photograph of these twins alive.

Chapter 20
Cyprus, Tuzla 1965

As the dry, short winter months drew to a close in Tuzla; Niyazi and Sevim materialized their plans to leave Cyprus and start their new life in England. Heartbroken and despondent, both were still mourning over their tiny, helpless son that they would soon leave behind. Sevim's attitude was more pragmatic, she would pack items up in the kitchen to prepare for her leaving. She knew that she would not and could not take anything with her. Niyazi enveloped his depression, heartbreak, and despondence. He concealed his tears so well that no single soul was able to notice his grief-stricken face whenever they stopped by Hamit Bey Sokak to pay their condolences. Hediye would stop by every day to help Sevim with cooking, tending to the goats and chickens, she could see Niyazi's grief and she knew he would open up perhaps in his own time.

Sevim struggled to breastfeed Hayriye notably since the experience in the hospital, it may have been Sevim's own grief that stopped her from producing any milk but bottle-feeding became harder. Every shop was now left empty and discarded of any baby milk or food items. Niyazi had closed the bakery before Christmas and the cafes were boarded up. Sevim found herself buying condensed milk to give to Hayriye

Sevim called Hediye over to ask her advice about feeding Hayriye. Hediye brought some oats together and started to leave it to boil; she added some molasses and a tiny amount of milk. She knew this type of porridge mixture wasn't optimal for a young baby but at least it would stop her from starving. This was Hayriye's diet for the next month along with the most basic vegetables, carrots and tomatoes that she dug out from the garden. Hayriye was on solids before her time, and Sevim felt reassured, her feelings of guilt for her son obviously transpired onto her daughter, and how she was looking after her. Sevim felt that she had made mistakes with Selcuk and her lack of confidence was self-evident. She relied heavily on Hediye, Hedi's way of putting Hayriye to sleep, Hedi's way of making Hayriye burp, Hedi's way of feeding her.

As the evening was ending and Hayriye was tucked up for her twenty-hour sleep, Sevim heard a gentle knock on the door. She knew it was Adnan who came over to run through the plans of their escape. Sevim had got accustomed to the spontaneous, splatter of bullets fired in an unknown street, and then the deafening silence of fear was the worst. How did this island go through so many changes in a short space of time? Sevim welcomed Adnan and Niyazi got up to pour a fresh, hot brew of Turkish tea.

That night Adnan explained more to Sevim than Niyazi, their plan to leave the island and start their lives in the UK.

'I will pick you up here at eight in the evening; we will drive to Lefke (Gemikonagi).' He added. Niyazi interrupted to explain further to Sevim their plans.

'You remember I told you about my school friend Suleyman.' He waited for Sevim to nod then continued, 'he worked with me in the bakery for years whilst my father was in prison. He lives in Lefke with his wife Ayşe and two children. We will stay there for one night and he will take us to the ferry port.'

Niyazi was about to pour Adnan a second glass of tea but Adnan lifted his head to signal no. Sevim interjected.

'This friend of yours, Suleyman, do you trust him?' She asked but his answer was simple.
'With my life!'

Niyazi's worry was not whether he trusted him or not it was the fact that Sevim had a Turkish passport and she could either be killed or sent back. He had a British passport so he knew he would use this. With the British military base in Lefkoşa Niyazi knew that there was a mutual respect for the military from both sides. If they could safely get on that ship, this would be their late and delayed, honeymoon dream, and start to their future.

Chapter 21
July 1965, Tuzla, Italy, Europe, UK

She clutched the hazed coloured pearls in her hands, is this what would become of her wedding dress, her dreams, and future? Sevim delicately tried once more to nip the dress into the only duffel bag she knew she couldn't bring. She asked Niyazi whether Adnan could sell the dress and send the money to them when they arrive in the UK.
'At least let me bring the gloves?' Sevim looked pleadingly into Niyazi's eyes. Niyazi always found it difficult to say no to anyone, and Sevim knew this. He nodded and gave an attentive smile that she became accustomed to. The gloves were made of a thin, white, muslin material, arm length, and had pearly white accompanied buttons on the side. Sevim felt a lot of emotions tonight; fear and anxiety were present, this was overtaken by the

excitement and thrill of seeing these cities in Europe. She had always dreamed about Italy, Milan, Venice, and London, only seen in "Ses" magazine. She would buy "Ses" magazine every month to look at knitting, crochet patterns, recipes, and photos of European cities that only famous actors and singers like Zeki Muran and Turkan Şoray would go to.

As the evening was drawing to a close; the sweet tangerine sky sunk to a close and Sevim enjoyed sitting out on the veranda that last time. She could smell the fresh lemons ripening on the tree and she pulled one off deciding to take it with her, she knew she wouldn't bring it all the way, she just wanted a temporary memory of being here in Tuzla.
 They heard Adnan's silent knock and crept out to the car. Sevim placed the tiny crib where Hayriye was sleeping in the back of the car. The lingering, twilight sky had dispersed into the distance leaving a silent, sombre evening. As the car smoothly rolled along, they were both aware of each other's silence but this time it wasn't deadly or eerie. For the first time in a long time, there seemed to be peace on the streets. In the summer of 1965, the situation in Cyprus was gradually worsening, Enosis was starting to become an important factor in Northern Cyprus, Makarios was trying to make sure that the bond and stable relationship between Greece and Cyprus were strengthening and this really left little time for Sevim and Niyazi to leave and find their path to freedom.
The journey to Lefka that evening was a solemn one, no one was in sight except for the oddly, stray dogs scratching their sides on the edges of roads and malnourished cats scuffling into the bins. On pensive evenings like this, you could only imagine something treacherous and ominous had happened or was about to.
 Niyazi could see Adnan was getting nervous, the shrunken cigarette hanging on his fingers was starting to fall and his shoulders were stooped as if he was hung in mid-air. Sitting at the back and gently caressing Hayriye's soft, auburn hair, Sevim broke the silence.
'How much further?'
 Without turning, Niyazi replied 'we're here; it's at the top here.'
Sevim remained calm, the road and pathway had dwindled into an overgrown, rural farm with the minuscule cottage in the distance metamorphosing into a dark, giant house in front of her eyes. She could see Suleyman and his wife signalling Adnan to park up close so the car could be hidden. Sevim questioned why anyone would come to such a solitary place but she knew the harbour was fairly near the distance.

Ayşe stood like a tiny, diminutive, chess piece next to Suleyman. She wore a black headscarf that matched the black slippers she had on. Her smile beamed from one ear to the other and she looked at Sevim with such sincerity, it was as if they had always been childhood friends. Her hands were on each daughters' head beside her. Sevim knew that for the children this would be the most exciting event to happen all week. Ayşe immediately took the crib inside and as soon as she let go, the girls flooded their arms around Sevim calling 'Sevim yenge' in unison.

Ayşe had already prepared a table of roasted chicken and pasta. The youngest, Sara intervened. 'Sevim yenge, sen Magarina bulli seversin?' Sevim looked at Niyazi in confusion. Up until this time she had never heard of the word bulli. She saw the chicken on the table with the lemon inside and knew this was Niyazi's favourite recipe but he had never called it bulli. As she glanced at Niyazi's eyes, she noticed him smirking. Sevim immediately nodded at Ayşe and she served a load immediately onto her plate.

Sevim left Niyazi and Suleyman to talk amongst themselves before she gave Hayriye a bowl of porridge so she could sleep. Ayşe offered her some milk but Sevim felt embarrassed, Hayriye had got used to this diet for four months now and she felt embarrassed to take any milk from them. She knew everyone was in the same situation; Suleyman was risking his and his family's life for Niyazi. Sevim knew how close they were, Niyazi had told her about how some of his Turkish Cypriots friends were turned in by Greek friends under Makarios' orders.

That evening seemed to run so slowly for Sevim, every second seemed like delayed time. Ayşe had made a bed for both of them on the floor using three huge blankets. Hayriye slept the whole night and Sevim woke her at six in the morning gently to feed her. Her eyes fluttered around at Ayşe's two children as they walked back and forth into the kitchen carrying the bread and cheese. She would curve her mouth to give a smile each time one would walk back, burp, and smile again. Her protruding cheeks were one of her grandmother's assets, Niyazi felt his mother's desperation to see her granddaughter but he had to be calm and rely on Suleyman.

Suleyman was now his saviour. Known around Lefke as a calm, peaceful man, his Greek was gently spoken and as good as his Turkish was. Ayşe piled more and more bread in front of them. She commented. 'You have to keep your strength up.' Even at times of danger people's customary values did not stop. Sevim had not realised till then how much determination and control they had as a family. Niyazi would tell Sevim about many Greek school friends he and Suleyman had and how they would share everything. 'There was a time' he would say 'we shared everything and never thought once about how we were different, we believed that it was what made

Cyprus so unique. There was no specific meaning or relevance why we would have learned two languages, we all did. It was nationalism that killed everything. As soon governments started believing that we were different, they would plant that seed into peoples' heads.' He spoke assertively and turned to Suleyman who nodded his head to signal 'it's time to go.' They placed their small belongings and the crib into Suleyman's Toyato Corona before heading off.

They left the path and Sevim noticed the streets had started to come to life again for the morning. It was fairly windy that morning, Sevim could see the palm leaves rustling against the pale, white buildings, Suleyman slowed down as he approached a shepherd in a long, thick coat. He wound the window down to greet him, the young shepherd lifted his cane to return the greeting. Suleyman proceeded through the market where everyone was about their own business. Sevim could see there were fragments of differences on this island but everything else remained the same. Three-wheeled carts haphazardly rattled along the cobbled path filled with pilavuna that a worn-out wife had obviously prepared the night before and a husband was ready to sell. Pockets of people were greeting one another as they entered the local Orthodox Church and further down, Sevim could see the copper and weaver markets. Old men would gather their strength to bash copper rimming into place, whilst weavers would delicately entwine horsehair into place. Baskets, trinkets, and stools hung outside. Sevim was in wonder; she felt she had been enclosed for the last year and a half. Niyazi chuckled at the front as he pointed to a young man carrying a cart of dead chickens. He added.
'You won't find that in London.' Sevim had obviously experienced Niyazi's market days when he would come back with a live tied chicken or octopus ready for its neck to be broken or beaten and thrashed to the floor. Suleyman turned off into various side streets to avoid the vendors and copper coffee pots laid out on rugs. Driving out of Lefka, Sevim noticed how near the sea they were. The car swerved around little alcoves, where silvery-white sails looked stagnant upon the water. Fishing boats rocked back and forth, whilst scraggy children were leaping into the tepid, turquoise water. It wasn't midday yet and Sevim saw this tiny hamlet come to life. Ahead she could see their journey. Their transport. The port had transpired into a busy pathway of soldiers, people in suits, families going on a similar journey as them, and workers loading large crates of potatoes on the Cyprus liner.
'This is it.' Sevim spoke as she propped herself up. 'This is where our journey begins.'

Suleyman swerved the Toyota around so they could walk up the ramp comfortably. As Sevim got out and took the crib, she noticed how calm everyone was. It looked as if everyone was going on holiday or a second honeymoon, it was impossible to see how slaughter was occurring around the island amongst this mellow place. Niyazi clenched Suleyman's arms like he was grabbing on to life, at that moment Suleyman slipped some folded money into his jacket pocket and Sevim now turned to Ayşe to thank her for helping them. They made their way onto the boarded ramp and looked back, their figures seemed like tiny Russian, babushka dolls beside one another.

They immediately went inside to find a seat and placed the crib under their feet. Sevim didn't want any issues with there being no ticket for Hayriye. Niyazi brought some Turkish tea and they sipped their tea in silence until they saw two ticket inspectors come forward. Sevim pushed the crib further back so it couldn't be noticed. The inspectors came forward and Niyazi took out the tickets and passports. The inspectors sifted through the tickets nodding and handing them back. They both stood momentarily looking at Sevim and her passport. Sevim looked at both of the inspectors and broke out.
'What's wrong sir with my passport?'
The inspector was taken aback that she had spoken but carried on looking and finally spoke.
'You have a Turkish passport ma'am, and you are on the Greek part of this island. You do realise we can turn the ship around and tell you to get off.'
Sevim by this time was fuming with anger and disbelief. Niyazi held her arm down as if to push her down but she was adamant to express her feelings.
'If it's not bad enough that there is a war going on around us, you want me to return to that place, she continued, 'I thought you didn't want me there, I thought you would be glad to get rid of another Turk.'
The officers looked around to see everyone's' stare in disbelief, they obviously didn't want to make a scene, closed the passports quickly then handed them back.
 Enjoy your trip' the officer announced and walked away.' Niyazi could see Sevim was still enraged, she felt her pride had been trampled on. 'How dare!' she declared but Niyazi still tried to calm her down.
It was undeniable that the officers preferred to have one less Turk to deal with rather than spend the rest of the afternoon cooped in an office filling in papers.
Towards the evening, both of them went outside on the deck with the crib to look at the sweltering, flare of the sky die down. They could see a

shadowing long line that resembled Salerno port and Sevim felt her whole body float into relief. They were finally starting their journey and letting go of all the carnage behind. Their melancholy was for the friends and family that they had to leave behind, their relief for the journey they had endured, and their happiness for what was about to begin for them.

(Niyazi on the ferry 1965 heading to UK)

Glossary

abla	a term of respect meaning big sister
ama	but
anne / annecim	a term for mother, mum
başınız sağolsun	may your head be healthy, a term used when someone close has died.
be	Oh god
bey	used after a name as Mr
Ben Ataturkciyim	I'm an Ataturk supporter

Boğazı Strait	the strait along the Bosphorus
bu	this
bulli	Cypriot term for chicken
büyük	big
Çay	Turkish tea
Dorma	stuffed vine eaves
Eğitim	education
Gazoz	fizzy lemonade drink in a bottle.
Gelin	bride
Helva	a type of sweet confection
Helim	halloumi cheese
Hoca	an Islamic Priest
Hun	a courtyard of shops
Jandarma	Turkish army
Kuruş	coin
Kim	who
koulouri, pilanuva, and helimli	types of Greek and Turkish Cypriot Bread
Lise	Lycee/ high school
mevlüt	a Islamic memorial service
Öf	ugh
O ne demek?	What does that mean?
Oğlum	son / my son
Salça	tomato paste
sen Kıbrız Turk değilmisin	are you not a Cypriot Turk?
Sevmek/ Severmisin	to like / do you like
Seftali sausage.	traditional Cypriot food. It is a type of
Su borek	a filling cheese pastry
Tespi	rosary
tütün	roll up tobacco in cigarettes

yenge   aunt

(Hayriye Osman Efendecikoglu)

Printed in Great Britain
by Amazon